This book belongs to:

My cocoon is:

by **RACHEL NOLEN**
and **MARIA PRICE**

The
COW
Cocoon

Pictures by
DAYNE SISLEN

Shoemaker Books
shoemakerbooks.stl@gmail.com

The Cow Cocoon

Library of Congress Control Number: 202 09 22 522
ISBN 978-1-7347831-0-0

Shoemaker Books

shoemakerbooks.stl@gmail.com

Acknowledgements

Dedicated to the loved ones in our cocoons:
Scott, Chelsea and Nick
Sara, Jack and Annie

We would also like to thank Dayne Sislen for her
wisdom and kindness.

Discover your Cocoon!
Visit us at www.cowcocoon.com

"It's here! It's here!" Truman exclaimed. The first day of spring had finally arrived. Mooma and Truman decided to celebrate by having a picnic.

Truman noticed a small pod hanging from a limb. "Mooma, what's that?"

"It's a cocoon." Mooma said. "A place where baby butterflies stay safe until they are ready to come out and play."

"Wow!" Truman said with amazement. "I wish I had a place like that! Mooma, do cows have cocoons?"

"Not really," she replied. "We have a barn."

"I wish we had a cocoon instead," Truman said.

Just then, Phil popped up. "I have a secret underground chamber! That's my cocoon."

Then, Jack hopped onto the blanket. "Howdy, Truman. My cocoon is my favorite hat. I keep it with me at all times."

Eager to join the conversation, Olivia hooted out, "I have a cocoon, too!"

"Chirp, chirp!" Carlos chimed in. "My cocoon is *un nido*, a nest."

Mooma giggled and said, "I guess a cocoon can be any special place that makes you feel safe, happy and loved."

After they finished their picnic, Jack asked Mooma, "Can Truman and I go down to the pond to play?"

"Of course!" Mooma said. "I'll meet you back here after my Udderly Yoga class."

Down by the pond, Truman saw his favorite frog friend. "Ingrid, do you have a cocoon?" he asked.

"*Ja, Ja,*" she croaked. "It's made of lily pads."

As they headed back up the hill, Truman thought about all of his friends' cocoons. Oh, how he wished he had his own special place.

"Hey, slowpoke." Jack said. "I gotta hop on home to get my chores done. You should get along to meet your Mooma."

Just then, Truman had an idea!
The best idea!

He backed up,
closed his eyes.
took a running start and...

Truman blinked his eyes and heard a whisper.

"Hey, Truman. It's me, Freida, the firefly. Don't be afraid. I will turn on my light so you can see."

Truman was glad to see his friend. He felt cozy and happy inside the big bale of hay.

Thunder startled Truman awake.
A storm was coming!

Mooma's eyes swept across the field, but she
couldn't find Truman.

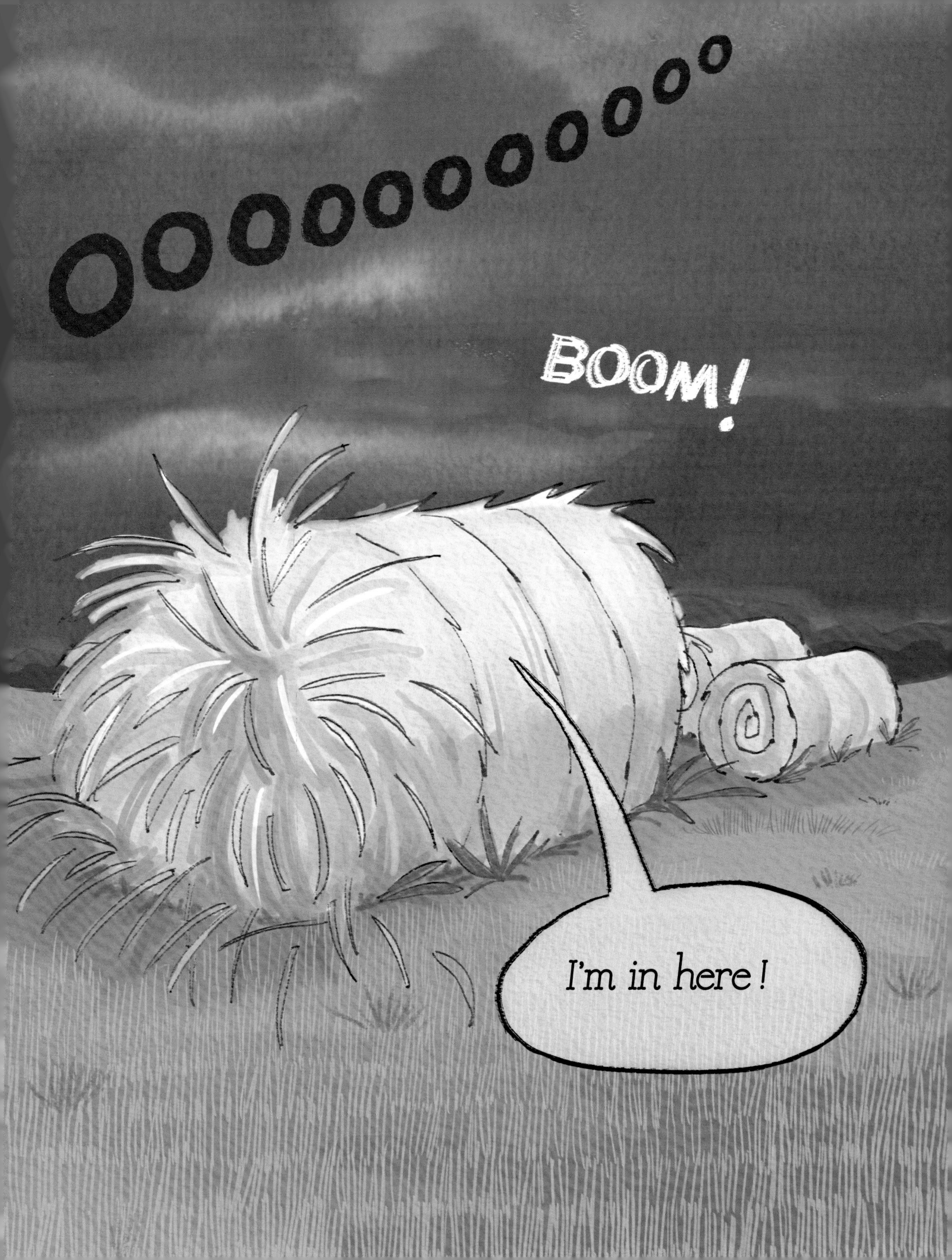
OOOOOOOOOOOOOO
BOOM!
I'm in here!

Relieved to see Truman, Mooma said, "I am
so happy that you are safe." She then gave
him a big nuzzle and a great, big lick.

"Mooma, I found my cocoon! I know it
because I felt so safe and happy there."

"That's wonderful!" Mooma said. "You can put
some of your favorite things in there after
the storm is over."

"That's a great idea!" Truman said. "I will put
my blankie, my teddy bear and maybe ..."

Mooma glanced up at the dark sky. "We need to get to the barn! The storm is here!"

Truman smiled when he saw that all of his family and friends were safely inside. "Mooma, this is our cocoon!" Truman said with glee. "And look who else found it!"

Mooma beamed with happiness and mooed. "We always have room in *our* cocoon."

Talking points:

We hope that you have enjoyed Truman's journey as he explored the meaning of 'cocoon.' We encourage you to talk to your children about their cocoons.

1. Where do they feel safe?
2. What does their cocoon look like?
3. What is in their cocoon?

This book illustrates that a cocoon can be any place that makes you feel safe. happy and loved. Use your child's imagination to create a cocoon. It can be made from anything and can take on any size and shape. For example. you can use a shoebox or oatmeal container. You can make a tent. or build a fort. Have fun as you explore the meaning of cocoon not only for your child. but for yourself!

Connect with us on Facebook or Instagram @thecowcocoon. We would love to see your creation.

Please visit us at www.cowcocoon.com to download activity pages.

Rachel and Maria

p.s. Did you find the butterfly spot on Truman?

Shoemaker Books

shoemakerbooks.stl@gmail.com